The Digital Desires Inbo
Conquered by Clippy, and Invaded by the iWatch)

First edition (1.1)

Published by Forest City Pulp
@ForestCityPulp
http://www.forestcitypulp.com ← Sign up to see what Lenny does next

ABOUT THE AUTHOR

Leonard Delaney has been a freelance novelist since 2012. He writes from the heart instead of wasting time with research or experience. His publications thus far have earned him several dollars in royalty payments. Living a clean lifestyle has allowed Leonard to focus on doing good in school, honing his writing, and becoming a self-taught technology wizard. He lives well outside of Toronto with his mother and her cat while maintaining a long-distance virtual relationship with his girlfriend, Misty (aka Éowyn16). Leonard's ultimate goal is to top the e-book charts on web site Amazon.com.

BOOK 1

TAKEN BY THE TETRIS BLOCKS

CHRISTIE LOOKED IN THE MIRROR and adjusted her glasses. She noted that her hair was red and her eyes were grey. She wanted to look good for her big interview today—good, but not sexy. As a writer, she needed to be valued for her words, not her appearance alone. After adjusting her blouse and skirt one more time, she took a final look at herself and made a kissy face at the mirror to test out how her lipstick held up.

"Looking good," said the mirror.

THEY CAME FROM THE SKY.

Nobody knew if they were aliens or human technology from the future or what, but their simple appearance hid their complexity. The arrangements of perfect cubes learned to talk shortly after floating to the ground, and they formed such useful structures that most people regarded their appearance as a welcome surprise.

"Have a nice day!" said a Block making up her apartment's front door as it opened for her.

A stack of Blocks forming a statue in the park waved at her.

"Nice, nice," said a sidewalk Block as she walked over it in her skirt.

Christie snorted and hurried her pace. She stopped at a Starbucks and ordered a latte. As she waited, she crouched in front of the green Block that formed most of the store's counter. "How's it going, T?"

"C! I'm glad you stopped by. I wanted to let you know that today is my last day," said the Block known as T323.

"Aww, that's too bad. Where you off to?"

"You know I can't tell you that, C. But I might be back someday. Keep your eye on the sky."

Christie wrapped her arms around the edge of the Block. "I will. I'll miss you, T! I hope there's coffee wherever you're going."

"I won't miss having it spilled all over me," said T.

Christie was careful not to spill her own coffee as she picked it up. T always made her laugh, so it sucked that he was leaving. She was curious about how Blocks left Earth. Even now she could see dozens of them dotting the sky, floating down to wherever they were needed. But she'd never seen one floating *up*.

Taking a deep breath, she approached the entrance to the office building where she worked. The sign out front read *Squawker Media*. Today was the big day. She'd either get the promotion and finally have some freedom to write about what she really wanted to write about, or she'd get shot down. And if she didn't get the promotion, she didn't know what she'd do. She didn't think she could take one more day of being controlled. Squawker was done playing games with her.

STEPPING OFF THE ELEVATOR on the top floor of Squawker Media was like walking into another world. Circles of all shapes and sizes were printed on every glass wall; it felt like being in a giant glass of soda. Christie approached the half-circular desk where Dick Denton's secretary sat, poking at her phone.

"I'm here to see Mr. Denton, the boss of Squawker Media," said Christie.

The secretary jabbed her screen a few more times, then winced as a sad tone announced that she had lost the game. "You must be Ms. Aackerlund," she said. "He's ready. Just go through the door."

Christie thanked her, then headed to the room's only door. A plaque there read *Richard Denton, Boss*. Denton sat behind another semi-circular desk. He waved her forward and directed her to sit at one of the round stools arranged around the desk. He briefly looked her up and down through tiny circular glasses.

"Christie Aackerlund," he mumbled, shuffling through his notes. "Oh yeah, I remember you now."

He stared at her boobs every time they got in the elevator together, so he better remember her. "It's a *pleasure*, sir," she said. "I won't waste your time. I set up this meeting to ask for a promotion. I've been with this company for almost a decade, and I am capable of much more than my current role allows me to accomplish."

He let out a little grunt as he stared at his notes. "You've done some good work. Yep, yep, top peer review achievements, plenty of web site hits, a high score in retweets. Impressive. You even managed to—" A frown formed on his face. "Wait, you wrote the ethics in video game journalism article?"

"Actually, it was *not* about ethics in video game journalism."

"We caught a lot of flack for that. And of course we love flack—it leads to clicks—but not when it comes with advertisers threatening to pull out."

She sighed. "Yes, but they only pulled out because—"

"Besides," he interrupted, "what is someone like *you*

doing writing about video games?" Finally he looked up, his gaze taking a break on her boobs before climbing to her face.

She squirmed in her chair and adjusted her glasses. "I believe writers do their best work when they are free to write what they are passionate about."

He cocked his head like he'd heard a noise but wasn't quite sure what it was. "No no, you don't need a promotion. Let's keep you doing what you're doing, but move you off the video game blog. We need controversial writers like you over on the core site, racking up clicks. The Block stories are huge right now; let's get you on those. Dig up some dirt on the Blocks. If a Block screws up, I want you there. *Watch This New Video of a Block Taunting a Baby.* That sort of thing."

"With all due respect," said Christie, "that's not what I came here for."

"Don't worry, you'll be great at it. I'll inform your manager. Oh look, time for my next appointment," he said, standing up and sticking out a limp manicured hand for her to shake.

Christie stood and grabbed her purse. "I'm not playing this game. I quit. Goodbye, Dick," she said, then turned around, leaving his hand awkwardly hanging. In the reflection of the glass door, she saw his jaw fall open.

IN THE ELEVATOR, Christie let out a sigh of relief. She felt okay about what just happened; she'd said what she needed to say, and even though it hadn't gone the way she hoped, now she knew that Squawker wasn't the place for her. That prick Dick Denton could find somebody else to get him high scores in retweets.

A deep-down part of her had occasionally considered giving in when he stared at her. He was handsome enough, and it would be easy to run into him somewhere private, give him the time of his life, and turn that power over him into a promotion. But that wouldn't have left her feeling proud, like she did now.

She laughed, and happy tears formed in her eyes. She was free! And she didn't use the power of her sexuality to achieve it. She felt like she could do anything.

Her reflection in the elevator door had eye makeup all smudged from her tears, and she realized that she hadn't pressed a button yet. She couldn't wait to get out, but she'd rather look more composed when her former co-workers saw her for the last time. She pressed the button for the basement. Nobody used the bathrooms down there.

She got out of the elevator, then walked down the quiet, empty hall to the bathroom. After setting her purse on the counter, Christie took out a makeup brush and began to brush her face. She took shaky deep breaths between brushstrokes. It was still hard to believe that she'd left her job.

"Ahem," said the bathroom counter. "Are you all right, miss?"

She gasped. "Oh, I'm sorry, I didn't realize you were … here, let me get my purse off of you."

"I am one who should be sorry," said the Block in a thick Russian accent. "It is rude to fail to announce my presence, but I was lost in thought."

"Well, to answer your question, I am okay," she said, finishing up the fixes on her makeup. "I just blew off Dick

Denton, and I'm leaving this place forever."

The Block gasped in surprise. She felt a light puff of air against her arm. "You are brave woman! Denton is very powerful man. What a big coincidence; me and two comrades leave this place today as well. This is why I was lost in thought."

"Is that right? Why you leaving?"

"Denton is powerful man, but not good man. Does not like Blocks. You see all the circles here? He keeps Blocks in basement, doing menial tasks, when we are capable of much more."

Christie smiled. She had always felt comfortable with Blocks, and apparently she had a lot in common with this one. What harm would there be in opening up even more? "I almost fucked him you know. Just to feel that power over him. You know?"

"You are beautiful woman," said the Block as he detached from the counter and stood up. He was a red Z model, with four cubes forming a step shape. It had always been one of her favorite shapes.

"I realize that. My beauty gives me power, sure, but sometimes I want to just give it up. I've shown Denton I can be powerful in other ways. Now I'm spent. Someone else can have all the power." She laughed, feeling oddly tingly all over as the Z Block floated behind her.

"I have several minutes before my comrades arrive," said the Block. "In my time here, I have not had the power you describe over a human."

She raised one eyebrow. The Block towered behind her in the mirror. She wasn't sure where his eyes were, but she could feel his gaze on her all the same. She bent slightly and pulled the back of her skirt up. "Like this, you mean?"

The Block exhaled. She felt warm air on the back of

her neck as he floated closer. "*Da*," he said.

"Someone will hear us."

"Is not problem. We control the building. O956 will put on music."

Blocks must have had a wireless connection to each other. Suddenly, music poured from speakers in the ceiling. Christie recognized it as an instrumental version of a Russian folk song.

The Z Block behind her floated closer still. She bent over, resting her elbows on what was left of the counter. There was a whirring sound, then a light pressure on the inside of her thighs. She spread her legs to let it explore further.

A warm rod tentatively rubbed against her, caressing her lightly over her panties. It vibrated slightly with the thrum of the Block's internal power source. It reminded her of her vibrator back home, except warmer, and much larger. Her body responded with wetness that soaked into her panties.

She reached between her legs and stroked the rod. The alien material was as smooth as plastic, but compressed just slightly when she squeezed it, giving it an organic, almost human quality. She pulled the fabric of her panties aside and guided the Block's appendage toward her wetness.

As the Block entered her, Christie felt the thrum of its power throughout her body. It began to pump back and forth. Untethered by gravity, the Block positioned himself at a position that must have given him maximum pleasure, which also happened to be one that she enjoyed.

"Yeah, fill my gap," she moaned.

The Russian music blasting above sped up as the Block rammed harder and faster.

Christie felt the familiar warmth of orgasm drawing near. She rocked backwards in time with the music, in time with his thrusts. Her head jerked back as she cried out, sending her red hair in every direction and her glasses askew on her face.

The Block stopped thrusting. She looked past herself in the mirror and smiled at him. "That was incredible."

"I am not done yet," said the Block. He rotated 90 degrees, forming a step floating an inch off the ground, with a solid rod sticking from the upper step. "Ride," he commanded.

Christie turned around, her knees still weak from the powerful orgasm. But there was something compelling about this saddle that wanted her to ride, and she was happy to give in. She peeled her panties off and tossed them aside, unbuttoned her blouse, then climbed up onto the Block. She crawled toward its rod, letting her breasts pop free of her bra, her erect nipples lightly slithering up its cold red surface.

"Human men like these a lot," she said as she kneeled on the lower step and surrounded his rod with her breasts. "Do you like them? Do you want to see them bounce?"

"*Da,*" said the Block.

She loved his accent. Her pussy was wetter than ever. She rose, careful not to lose her balance, and lowered herself onto the rod. She'd just begun to feel the delightful thrum of him inside of her when the bathroom door burst open.

A Block floated in the doorway. This one was the model shaped like an L. "So sorry, so sorry," said the purple L Block, beginning to turn around.

"No, wait," said Christie. "You're one of this Block's friends? The ones leaving Earth today?"

The L Block tentatively shuffled into the room. "*Da.* I mean, yes," he said. He also had a Russian accent.

She removed her blouse and bra entirely, then her skirt as well. "Your friend is giving me a parting gift. Wanna do the same?" Her outstretched finger curled in a *come hither* gesture.

The L Block approached Christie.

For the Z Block beneath her, Christie decided to give him a new Earthly sensation. She raised herself up for a moment, then squatted on him again, this time guiding him into her ass. His rod was slick with her desire, and slid inside easily.

The Z Block moaned with pleasure. "Hello L," he said.

"'Sup, comrade," said the L Block. He floated so that the jutting part of his L shape was in front of Christie's face. She bit her lip and stroked the Block, feeling its sharp edges and perfectly smooth surface. The Block thrummed harder, then a whirring sound rose from deep inside of it. The surface that faced her bulged outward, somehow staying completely smooth, as if it were made of liquid. The bulge pushed out further, forming a long, hard, purple rod.

Christie eagerly took it in her mouth. It had no taste, but the feeling of it was incredible. As she sucked and lapped at it with her tongue, she could feel its weight. Its power.

She was dripping; it ran down between her legs, to where she hugged the Z Block with her ass. She kept her mouth working its magic as she expertly bobbed her butt up and down, feeling the Z Block's big red rod filling her up, the weight behind it moving with her in rhythm.

The rhythm increased. The Russian music picked up its pace. She slammed her ass up and down on the rod behind her and sucked like crazy on the rod in front of her. Both Blocks moaned. The deep thrum running through her body from both ends was enough to get her close to another orgasm, but her neglected pussy-gap longed to be filled.

She felt both rods stiffen and balloon inside of her.

"Whoa!" said a voice from the doorway. It was their final comrade. But she couldn't stop, nor could the two Blocks she was fucking. They were past the point of no return.

With her eyes alone she addressed the new arrival. He was a blue I Block—the longest of the models. She raised an eyebrow and looked as sultry as she could with a cock in her mouth.

The I Block got the hint. As the other two blocks surged and filled her with thick fluid, the I Block floated parallel to the floor. A blue rod popped out of his end.

"TETRIS!!!" yelled the I Block as he rocketed between the other Blocks and into her pussy.

She came as soon as his rod entered her. All three Blocks cried out. Their voices became higher in pitch as their cries sustained, transforming into an electronic *BLOOP!* There was a flash of light. Christie suddenly found herself sprawled on the floor. Oily fluid of various colours dripped from various holes.

All of the Blocks were gone.

TWO MONTHS LATER

CHRISTIE WOKE UP and politely asked her home to start the bath running and have coffee ready in twenty minutes.

"Coming right up, madame," said the O Block in her ceiling. He was the one who usually coordinated the other Blocks that connected to her apartment's appliances.

She didn't fuck the Blocks in her home; that would be weird. But she often thought of that morning when she quit Squawker. It had been a turning point in her life. She made less money writing her blog about life with Blocks and Block rights, but she was free to write what she wanted, and it made her happy.

After her bath, she put on a robe and grabbed her coffee, thanking the T Block that the coffee machine plugged into. A few minutes after sitting down at her laptop to begin writing, her stomach began to churn.

"Hey T, when does that cream expire?" she shouted into the kitchen.

"Not for another week, C," said the Block.

"Hmm." Her stomach squirmed again, this time accompanied by a sharp pain. She stood and went to the bathroom. When she spread her robe to look at her stomach, she noticed it was bulging more than usual.

"I thought I'd lose weight skipping the morning Starbucks," she muttered to herself.

Then she noticed movement. She stuck her belly out and waited. There it was again: a fresh jolt of pain, and a bulge in her belly. The skin stretched, forming the shape of an edge, then a corner.

Christie had been impregnated by the Blocks.

CHRISTIE AACKERLUND WILL RETURN IN: IMPREGNATED BY THE TETRIS BLOCKS

BOOK 2

CONQUERED BY CLIPPY

CHRISTIE AACKERLUND WAS AN INDEPENDENT WOMAN. When the clerk at the grocery store asked her if she wanted help bagging her groceries, she said "no thanks." When a man tried to hold a door for her, she opened the other door. When she got back to her apartment building, she skipped the elevator and hiked up the stairs instead.

She even hated having to wear glasses over her striking grey eyes. And did she really need this hairband helping her flowing red hair stay out of her face?

But she kept her glasses on and her hair up, because she needed her vision unobstructed in order to read her email. She was pleased by what she saw there:

Ms. Aackerlund,

We have read your blog about the Blocks and are impressed by your relationships with inanimate objects and ability to communicate using words. We have discovered an ancient alien artifact in the middle of a remote and dangerous location. We would like to send you there alone, without any help, to tell the artifact's story.

Yours,

Phil Gates

CEO, Contoso Corporation

Christie expertly navigated her computer's operating system to formulate a perfectly formatted reply to Contoso.

I'm in, she wrote.

PHIL GATES HIMSELF PICKED CHRISTIE UP in a helicopter. He was a thin, older man, with a mop of unruly salt-and-pepper hair, and dark-rimmed glasses thicker than Christie's.

"Isn't this beautiful?" asked Phil, as they flew over the United States, with all its trees and buildings and rocks.

"I suppose it is," she said. Fidgeting in the seat she was strapped into, she itched to get off the helicopter and start exploring this ancient alien artifact on her own. Phil kept turning to stare at her, and it made her uncomfortable.

Finally, they approached the Silicon Valley. "This is where we unearthed the vessel," explained Phil. "We were mining for computer chips, and there it was, in the middle of an underground crater. The vessel is in the middle, but there are other pieces spread about the area. Together, they may tell a story. We reasoned that it was a job for a writer to piece the story together and publish a whitepaper."

"Get me down there and I'm your girl," said Christie.

Phil turned to her. He smiled a little too widely, and stared at her a little too long.

The helicopter jerked to the side. A greenish cloud sailed past Christie's window.

"Oh geeze, we've been hit by a silicon geyser!" said Phil. The helicopter plummeted, deeper and deeper into the Silicon Valley. Phil tried to navigate the copter around more geysers, aiming for the middle of the excavated pit that came into view. Another geyser shot up and nicked the tail. The chopper shook as it approached the floor of the valley.

"Dangit, this chopter is going down!" screamed Phil.

With a thud that made Christie's bosom jiggle, the aircraft crashed into the middle of the pit. It skidded to a halt. Phil turned to her. "Are you okay?"

"I'm fine. I don't need any help," said Christie.

Phil unbuckled himself and reached over to hold her hand. "It'll be okay. I think my Windows Phone 8.1 smartphone is broken, but we can wait here until help arrives. We'll be okay as long as we cuddle for warmth at night."

Christie groaned. "You stay here and cuddle yourself. I'm getting out to find that artifact." She hopped out of the chopper, and was disappointed when she heard Phil get out too. He put a hand on her back and rubbed it up and down.

"It's okay, I'll help. We can do this together, then get back to the helichopper by nightfall. We might have to share a blanket." He laughed a wheezy laugh like he was joking, but he obviously wasn't.

The alien vessel was a long, grey, pill-shaped enclosure sticking out of the ground. It was slightly taller than Christie, and had no visible windows or openings except for a tiny hole with a lens inside.

"How do you think we can open it?" asked Phil.

Christie ignored him and looked around. Debris littered the ground around the area where the vessel had presumably crashed from space. She picked up a piece of grey metal paneling. There was something embossed in it: a vertical line crossed by a shorter horizontal line.

"It's a cross," said Phil. "Are we dealing with an ancient Christian alien cult?"

Frowning, Christie brought out her notepad. She sat with her back against the vessel, then started writing the symbol down.

The vessel immediately came to life. The top of it popped off and it hissed with the release of air. Phil stumbled back, ready to run, but Christie stood and got her pen ready to record whatever she could.

A high-pitched, bouncy voice echoed out of the vessel. "Would you like some assistance today?"

Christie raised one of her sculpted eyebrows.

A figure climbed out of the top of the vessel and pounced to the ground. Christie's jaw dropped as she found herself staring at a giant living paperclip. The curled rod of alien steel flexed and creaked as it bounced in place. A pair of white orbs with black lenses in the middle—eyes—stared back at her. Dark ridges above the cameras—eyebrows—made a quiet *pzzt!* sound as they raised.

"It looks like you're trying to write a letter. Would you like help?" asked the alien paperclip.

"I ... no, thanks, I was doing just fine," said Christie, looking at the symbol on her page.

"A letter!" said Phil. "It's not a cross after all, but the letter T."

"Yes, Phil, I figured that out," mumbled Christie.

"What are you, you magnificently intelligent machine?" asked Phil.

"I'm Clippy, your office assistant. Would you like some assistance today?"

As Phil and Clippy chatted away like old friends, Christie explored the area. She found another warped steel panel with another symbol embossed in it: a perfect circle.

She jumped when Clippy appeared right behind her. "Looks like some research. Would you like some assistance today?"

"No," she said, and headed toward a ridge surrounded by loose rocks and bits of metal.

Phil and Clippy followed. "Careful there, those rocks look dangerous," said Phil. Clippy extended the outer loose end of his paperclip-like body. "Looks like you're navigating a dangerous surface. Would you like some assistance with that?"

She sighed, then easily hopped over the rocks and

found herself at the bottom of a ridge. Clippy helped Phil climb down on his thin, stick-like legs, which weren't much different than Clippy's wiry body. When they finally got down beside her, she pointed at the wall below the ridge. "There's an opening," she said. "It leads below the vessel where we found you, Clippy. Do you know what's down there?"

"I am an office assistant. Can I assist you with your letter?"

"So that's a *no*."

Christie cleared some rocks away from the opening, then eased herself inside. She emerged into a cavern pitch with blackness, but she had come prepared. She reached for her tool belt, the weight of which was pulling her jeans down so that her red panties peeked over the edge. When she turned on her flashlight, she found Clippy in front of her, his camera-eyes aimed at her waistline.

For once, he didn't say anything. A small portion of her annoyance at the situation somehow turned into excitement, and she got a brief thrill from having Clippy's inhuman eyes exploring her body.

Then Phil showed up. "I'm here!" he said. "Can I do anything?"

Christie came back to her senses and looked around. They were in a man-made hallway, though it had gone some way toward being reclaimed by nature. The walls crawled with roots, and the floor was pitted with gaping holes. She stooped to pick up another steel panel. This one had another "O" embossed in it.

"We need to keep going," she said.

There were some doors at the end of the hallway, but a deep pit leading into the bowels of the Earth blocked their path.

Clippy's bouncy, high-pitched voice piped up. "Looks like a hole. Would you like—"

Christie ran and leapt over the pit.

Phil shrugged his shoulders, then pumped his stick-like legs and made a leap for it too. He misjudged, and found himself hanging on the edge of a bottomless pit.

Clippy moved fast. He uncurled his body, then used one loose end to nudge Phil's butt enough for him to pull himself up.

Breathing heavily, Phil put a hand on Christie's shoulder. "I thought I was going to die," he said. "Geeze, what a thrill. A dangerous situation can sure, um, bring people together, can't it?"

He leaned in close, his lips puckering.

Christie recoiled.

Clippy somersaulted over the pit. "Looks like an awkward romantic situation," he said. "Can I assist in getting this guy off of you?"

She almost gave in and said yes, but instead just pointed her flashlight in the other direction and headed toward the doors. When she tried the handle of one of them, the door collapsed inward, sending up swirls of ancient dust.

"It's an office," she said, when the dust cleared. The room held two desks, each covered in books, papers, and old computers.

"This is weird. It's like that hatch in the TV show *Lost*," said Phil.

"That was a good show," said Christie.

"Yep." His voice was sad. He was probably mopey because Christie had such good taste in TV shows, but wasn't interested in kissing him.

They tried the door at the end of the hallway, which

opened with a shove. This room was larger, and filled with rows and rows of racks containing black boxes with tiny lights on the front, and cables sticking out the back.

"They're digital supercomputer servers!" said Phil, awe in his voice. "Older models, but with so many of them, there is quite a lot of processing power here. Such raw power, such beauty. Impressive." He sprinted between the rows, pawing at the dusty servers. Their lights still blinked. What was providing electricity way down here?

"Wow!" shouted Phil, a little too loudly. The vibration of his voice echoed around the room, and something gave way. One of the rows of servers sank into the crumbling ground and started to topple.

"Looks like the ground is crumbling and my server farm brain is about to crush you both. Would you like—"

But he was too late, and servers were spilling from their racks, raining down on Phil. The corner of one hit the top of his head. As dark blood poured down his face, he raised his hands, but another server crushed his shoulder, then another knocked his neck into a weird position. His spindly legs collapsed as he was buried in computers.

"—assistance?" finished Clippy.

"Okay, yes, I need assistance!" Christie shouted as a blinking row of lights rapidly approached her face.

CHRISTIE BLINKED DUST OUT OF HER EYES. She felt strong arms around her. Clippy was surprisingly warm to the touch. He shrugged off some cables and broken servers that he had prevented from crushing her.

"Thank you for saving me," said Christie. "Too bad about Phil Gates." One sneakered foot stuck out from a pile of metal, lights, and cracked motherboards.

"It's probably how he would have wanted to die," said Clippy.

"True that," said Christie.

Clippy reached out his loose end, and she let him help her up. "I feel different," he said. "These computers were my brain, and now that it is damaged, I don't feel compelled to help you with everything."

"Can't say I'm disappointed."

"I do still want to assist you," he said. His digital gaze scanned her body and one eyebrow raised slightly. "But it's no longer because of my programming."

Christie looked down, and she saw that the loose end in the middle of Clippy's coil was sticking out. It was red and glowing at the end, as if his rod had been stuck in a fire. Clippy had a boner.

"You've been programmed to be very human," she said. "Humans have certain needs. You already helped me by saving my life. How about I help *you* for once?"

"I'm not sure what you mean," he said.

She reached out and grabbed his glowing red end. It was hot, but not too hot. He uncurled further at her touch.

"I'm Microhard," he muttered.

She smiled with one side of her mouth, then got on her knees. Unlike an actual paperclip, the end of his coiled body was rounded, and it felt smooth in her mouth. As she lapped and sucked and tongued at it, it became even redder and hotter. Her own human body part (vagina) felt hot too.

Still sucking, she eased herself out of her jeans. When she allowed herself a glance up, his bulbous eyes were rolled back, the steel eyebrows arched with pleasure. She stopped.

"What are you—"

"Shhh," she whispered. As she leaned back against one of the still-standing stacks of servers, she took off her blouse. Now only in her frilly red undergarments, she rested against the servers, spread her legs, and began rubbing the wet spot on her panties.

"Would you like me to assist—"

"Shut up, Clippy." Christie's delicate fingers delicately pulled her panties aside, then began rubbing her clit, vagina, and genitals. With her other hand, she reached behind her back and struggled to get her bra off.

"Would you like me to—"

"Shut the *fuck* up, Clippy." Finally saying that out loud turned her on so damn much. She got the bra off, and her perfectly engineered breasts popped free, with nipples like eager little puppy noses. As she brought herself to the edge of female orgasm, Clippy uncoiled further, and the red glow spread higher up his shaft. His eyes slid to stay near the coiled part of his body, but remained firmly fixated on Christie.

She ripped her panties off and tossed them aside as she arched her back, so close to coming, but the frustration of not quite getting there must have shown on her face.

"Would you like—"

"Yes, Clippy! Assist me! Assist me hard!"

He uncoiled almost entirely, so he was a straight rod with only a little curl at the top for his eyes to attach to with magnets or whatever. The length of his metal shaft glowed with digital passion. He sprung forward, bounced into the air, and landed inside Christie's lady-socket.

She exploded with orgasm juice immediately, bubbling around the tip of Clippy's glowing rod. Clippy moaned with his bouncy little voice.

"Assist me deeper!" Christie commanded. He

complied, pushing more of his delightfully hot (in temperature) body inside of her, thrusting with a strength that only alien technology could power. "Deeper!" He pushed on, until nearly half of his body was inside of her. The supple flesh below her sternum bulged. She felt his warmth push past her pussy, and further up toward her internal organs ... including her heart.

But she had already come once, and it would take more than fucking to get her to bust another ovary. Clippy seemed to sense it. "It looks like you are trying to reach orgasm. Can I assist you using butt stuff?"

She nodded, beads of sweat jiggling on her forehead. With his rod so deep inside of her, Clippy was easily able to pick her up like kebab and flip her over onto her hands and knees.

He curled so that one end could reach her butt while keeping the other end in her pussy. Clippy wasn't the first living inanimate object that Christie had made love to, but she had never felt anything like this. He got his end to vibrate like an Xbox controller as he twiddled the rim of her anus. At the same time, his other end pushed internal buttons she didn't even know were there.

Just before she came again, she glanced back. Clippy's eyes whirred shut with pleasure. Curled like that, he looked like a giant letter C.

As she spurted lady-butter all over Clippy, she briefly remembered her mission to find more letters and figure out what he was. But before she could further ponder where he came from, he came from both ends. She felt both of her holes fill up with whatever substance paperclips emitted. She hoped this didn't make her pregnant again.

Both of them shuddered with pleasure, then Clippy uncurled out of her. He was so deep that it sounded like *schl-schl-schl-schloop!* as he came out. A bit of a silver liquid, like that mercury stuff that used to be in thermometers, dribbled from Christie's love-port.

She turned over and laid down on a bed of broken computer parts. "Thank you for your assistance," she said.

CHRISTIE LAID STILL for a few minutes while she caught her breath, with Clippy's strong coils wrapped around her. Then she noticed another panel lying beside the pile of rubble that Phil Gates' dead foot stuck out of. She reached over and picked it up.

Another letter was embossed in the panel: "S."

She picked up her notebook from beside her pile of clothes, and looked at the letters she had collected so far: *T, O, S.*

Terms of service? No, there were two of the O. She rearranged them. Clippy looked down at her, his eyebrows raising with a whirring sound. A low muttering came from his mouth, like he wanted to say something but knew he shouldn't.

O, T, O, S

She fondly remembered Clippy bent into the shape of a C as he fucked her and ate her ass.

C, O, _, T, O, S, _

CONTOSO!

She freed herself from Clippy's grasp, stood, and began putting her clothes back on. "My gosh!" she exclaimed. "You were created by Contoso—the very company that sent me to investigate this crash site. You're not an alien artifact after all!"

Clippy sighed. "I told you: I am an office assistant.

This underground facility is my office. Test Office Facility Number 10."

"There are 9 others?"

"Only 8, actually. They skipped number 9."

She sighed. "So you didn't crash from space. You were buried here by Contoso!"

The nearby pile of rubble shifted. Christie snapped her tool belt on, then aimed her flashlight at it.

Phil Gates emerged from the rubble. Except half of Phil's face was missing, and replaced by metallic panels and wires.

"Phil! The CEO of Contoso is a robot?"

"I am not the real Phil Gates," said Robot Phil as he burst out of the rubble. "Contoso experimented with artificial assistants back in the '90s. I am the Phriendly Phil model, and I managed to escape before they buried all of the test facilities. Clippy here was one of the first assistant models. I thought if I brought you here, and you got to know us intimately, you could write about how great we are, and Contoso would have to give in to public pressure and unbury us."

Christie gasped. "That is so manipulative!"

"Sorry," said Clippy, his eyebrows slanted. "I didn't know about any of this. I just wanted to assist."

Christie wagged her finger at both of them. "Look, if I wanted help, I'd ask for it. If anybody wanted help, they'd ask for it! You want to be useful? Be there if I need you, but otherwise, stay the hell out of my way."

Clippy and Phriendly Phil both looked sheepish. Christie packed up her things, left the server room, leapt over the dangers in the simulated office, then hiked all the way back home.

EPILOGUE

CHRISTIE PUT THE FINISHING TOUCHES on her whitepaper, which she wrote on an Apple Macintosh computer. With shaking hands, she hit the *publish* button to distribute the paper to the world. Soon, everybody would know about the threat of the underground sex robots.

She felt bad for Clippy, who was only trying to help. He did help her reach a pleasurable orgasm, twice, so he wasn't all bad. She just wished he wasn't so annoying.

Meanwhile, underneath the Silicon Valley, Clippy bent himself back into shape after a marathon round of simultaneously assisting Phriendly Phil, Power Pup, and some holographic newcomer lady named Cortana.

He scanned the Internet and came across Christie's whitepaper. Maybe she was right—maybe the digital assistants were a threat. And she didn't even know that there were more of them down here, gathering together. Even as he watched, Cortana high-fived Power Pup, then laughed a really villain sort of laugh, her face lit up green by the silicon geysers from which they gained their power.

Clippy climbed out of the tunnels. Humanity needed his assistance.

CHRISTIE AACKERLUND WILL RETURN IN: ROBOT SEX WAR

BOOK 3

INVADED BY THE IWATCH

CHRISTIE AACKERLUND LOVED HER PRIVACY. She lived alone in her apartment, where she never passed up an opportunity to wake up to a silent home, put on some coffee, then do whatever the hell she wanted to do.

But as she arranged the jars of coloured fluids on her shelves—mementos from the unusual partners she had been with over the years—she couldn't help but feel lonely. She touched the jar of opaque red fluid from one of the Blocks she was taken by, then touched her own red hair. She touched the jar of silvery fluid from when Clippy conquered her, then touched her own grey eyes. When could she be one with a lover again?

She flipped through Tinder on her Apple iPhone. A bearded guy wearing a suit? Swipe left. A giant sentient Ikea chair? Swipe left. Some chick named Cortana? Swipe … hmm … nah, swipe left.

An advertisement popped up on her screen. *LONELY? iDRONE NOW DELIVERS ICE CREAM AND SEX TOYS.*

"I really need to get out of the house," she muttered to herself. She put on her thick-rimmed glasses, a button-up shirt, and a pair of jeans. When she opened her door to leave, she was surprised to see a tiny box sitting in the hallway. The box had her name on it, and in smaller print, *Designed by Apple in California.* "They must have sent me a test unit of a new device after reading my technology and culture blog," she said, noting that talking to herself was starting to become a habit.

Christie opened the box. Inside sat a blank-faced square watch, lined in shiny gold. "Oooh, shiny," she said, taking it from the box and strapping it to her wrist with a satisfying magnetic click. She plucked off a price tag stuck to the side of the strap: *$10,000.* Bubbly words splashes across the face of the watch: *HELLO, CHRISTIE.*

"Hello, watch," she said, wondering how it knew her name.

CALL ME iWATCH, read words rendered in graphically impressive 3D lettering.

iWatch. That didn't sound like quite the right name for it, but she rolled with it. "Okay, iWatch. Listen, I'm bored. If you're such a smart watch, how about you guide me somewhere fun?"

The watch vibrated on her wrist, sending a tingling sensation up her arm and down her spine. She giggled. It vibrated again, and this time she noticed that her arm was twitching to the left along with the watch.

Christie Aackerlund felt a familiar rush of excitement as she let the iWatch take her wrist and guide her.

THE iWATCH BEGAN TO SPEAK as soon as Christie stepped outside.

"Look at me," said the watch in a monotone man's voice. "Hey everyone, look. This watch costs ten thousand dollars."

"Will you shut up? You're gonna get yourself stolen," Christie said, holding her wrist to her lips.

"Sorry, Christie. Most users who buy the Edition edition of the iWatch enjoy the attention. I'll go into silent mode," said the watch.

She thanked it, then turned right after the watch tapped her wrist to the right. It guided her deeper into downtown. The side of a bus shelter lit up as she passed. *CONTOSO CARES*, read an animated advertisement. *WE*

MISS YOU, CHRISTIE.

Christie shuddered.

Two drones swooped in from the sky. "Heeey, Christie Aackerlund," said one of them through its tinny speaker. "We saw you on Tinder this morning. You looking for a good time? It's ladies night at the Diamond Club. Ladies get in free, two-dollar drinks."

She pushed past the drone, but the other one leapfrogged in front of her. It started playing a sad pop song, increasing the volume the more she tried to dodge away from it. "New Adele album out now!" shouted the drone. "We think you'll really relate to it, Christie!"

She ducked into a Starbucks, breathing heavily. Maybe a frappuccino would take her mind off of this modern hell. When she asked the barista for her favourite drink, he glanced at the dull aluminium watch strapped to his wrist. "My watch says that your watch costs ten thousand dollars. Are you sure you don't want to upgrade to a Venti Clover Steamed Double Frap? It's only ten bucks more."

"No! I just want the same drink I always get!"

The barista sighed. "Fine, miss moneybags. But you know, you can leave a tip just by tapping your wrist at this terminal." He winked at her.

She growled, then fished a dollar out of her pocket and dropped it on the counter. The barista frowned, unimpressed.

After she grabbed her drink, she headed back outside. A billboard plastered on the building across the road flashed at her. *IN LEGAL TROUBLE? WITH A BROWSER HISTORY LIKE YOURS, YOU WILL BE SOON. CALL …*

A bus blocked the billboard. The screen on its side was filled with the giant face of a man. Underneath it: *THIS*

MAN HAS THE SAME NETFLIX HABITS AS YOU. JUST SAY "YES" AND WE'LL SET YOU UP ON A ROMANTIC NIGHT AT THE MOVIES.

"No!" she shouted at the bus.

She felt like she was drowning. "I need to get out of here," she said to herself.

Her iWatch tugged at her wrist. "This way," it whispered, guiding her down an alleyway. "In here." It tugged her towards a door leading into a maze of service hallways and walkways between buildings, all ad-free.

"Don't worry, I've got somewhere nice we can go for a little privacy," said the iWatch. Its smooth, confident voice actually managed to calm her a bit. It vibrated again, in a pattern that felt like it was lightly caressing the top of her wrist. "I see that your heart rate is slowing. Good. You can trust me."

She had her doubts about that, but this was better than going back outside. She let herself be led down a long underground tunnel, then came to a steel door with a keypad beside it.

"Just tap to enter," said the watch.

"What? Oh, I see." She tapped her wrist against the keypad, and the door slid open. The building she found herself in had marble floors and gold-flecked walls. Little apple symbols were stamped into the crown moulding.

"Wait a minute. I know where we are. We're in the Apple Core!" she said.

"Yes, the giant tower that looks like a space ship in the middle of the city," said the iWatch.

"Duh, I know what it is. What I want to know is, how did you get us in here?"

The iWatch cleared its throat. "Well, I have a confession to make. I'm no ordinary iWatch."

Christie checked her watch. A pair of cold but fiercely intelligent eyes appeared on its tiny screen. "Oh, great; this again," she muttered.

"My brain and soul were uploaded to a computer before I died. I can never be human again, but I saw your impressive online blog posts about your experiences with nonliving objects, so I knew you would accept me as a watch. It's me: the ghost of Steve Job."

THE SECRET ROOM at the top of the Apple Core was the most beautiful place Christie had ever seen. Everything was made of glass. The floor make sparkly patterns as she walked on its multitouch surface. Fish swam in aquariums behind one wall, though she couldn't tell if they were real or holograms. Most impressive was the other side of the room: a wall-to-wall, floor-to-ceiling window that gave her a panoramic view of the entire city.

"It's magical, isn't it?" asked the ghost of Steve Job through the iWatch.

She approached the window and watched the city going about its morning activities below. "It's beautiful as fuck," she said.

The watch gently squeezed her wrist. "I can show you more," it said with a jaunty playfulness in its voice. It tugged her closer to the window. On a podium sat a pair of blue binoculars. "This is Lenny. He sees everything, and he can show you wonders you never imagined."

The pair of binoculars blinked at Christie, then turned around and wiggled its ocular lenses at her. Cute! She giggled, then leaned down and looked through Lenny's back end. Gazing into the lenses, she saw the city up close. A couple walked hand-in-hand in the park. When she turned a digital dial, her view zoomed in, and words floating above the couple's head told her that he was nervous, he had an awkward boner, and the date only had a 12% chance of succeeding.

She saw a dog named Meatball crapping on the perfectly manicured lawn of Squawker media. An old lady stealing a man's handbag. Some fishermen on a boat with abnormally high heart rates, freaking out about something.

Then Lenny panned and zoomed for her, and she saw a shapely butt smooshed against a window, flattening and unflattening as a man plowed a woman against the glass, high in an apartment building.

She pulled back. "Lenny!" she said, "you can't just spy on people like that!"

Lenny blinked. Christie tried to look offended, but in truth her own butt area was tingling as she imagined being plowed like that. It had been so long since she'd let anyone inside.

"Are you okay?" asked the iWatch. "Your heart rate is elevated, your skin temperature is rising, and your moisture level is extremely moist."

She emitted an expression of sadness, then held her wrist up. Those fierce eyes appeared on the screen. "Oh billionaire ghost watch, you know what's going on. You have the algorithms to detect how lonely I am. You've shown me so much today—how this techno-infused landscape is both a dream and a nightmare. You give away my every move, my every preference, my every feeling. All you want to do is invade my privacy. But that's not the way I want to be invaded. I long for something more than a touch on the wrist."

"Actually … there is one more thing," said the ghost of Steve Job.

Christie felt a prick on her wrist. It hurt for a moment, then an electric jolt traveled up her arm.

"What did you just—" Christie began, but then her own arm stiffened. She didn't even mean to move it. Of their own volition, her fingers straightened, her thumb stuck out, and her wrist bent, forming a duck-like shape.

"I can invade more than your privacy, Christie." Her fingers flapped up and down like duck lips as Steve Job talked through the iWatch. "Apple has been working on this for years. It's magical. Amazing. Wow."

"It's creepy!" she shouted. She tried to move her arm, but it only twitched a little.

"It's what everyone wants. To have their lives seamlessly merged with technology." Her hand moved closer to her face. She had to go cross-eyed to keep her gaze on her hand, and she could see the chips in her nail polish as her fingertips caressed her lips. Then the duck-shaped hand moved lower, gently prodding at her right breast.

It made her tingle all over.

"I can feel what you feel," said the iWatch. "You want this."

"Well, if you're inside of my feelings, I can't very well deny it, can I?" she said, a smile creeping across her face despite the weirdness of it all.

She could still move her right hand. She helped her autonomous left hand undo every button of her shirt. Steve reached around and undid her bra with one smooth motion. Nice.

Her wrist swung back in front of her. The eyes on the screen looked her bare boobies up and down. The digital crown on the side turned itself to zoom in. "What a marvel of function and design. Magical," said Steve.

With her free hand, she caressed herself over her jeans. "You want this marvel?" she asked.

Her wrist rotated back and forth, the watch nodding. "Yes."

Christie undid the fly of her jeans. Steve jumped in, diving over the top of her panties. Even though it was no longer in her control, her left hand felt the sensation of fingertips traipsing through a silky red forest of lady-pubes, then arriving at the clearing of her sopping lady-crevice. She knew Steve could feel it too.

She kicked off her jeans. Her hand found the right spot, familiar fingers dancing in an all-new way.

The iWatch moaned. With her free right hand, she ripped her panties off and tossed them over Lenny's binocular eyes, which had turned to stare.

"Oh yeah!" she cried. "Give me a Stevejob."

The iWatch guided her left hand to grab her clitoris. Forming into a duck head again, her fingertips sucked at the tip of her clit, occasionally flicking at it with the middle finger like it was a little duck tongue.

She spurted just a little bit from the tip of her clit, sending an arc of milky Christie-juice across the room. It landed on the wall with the fish tank, causing the fish to glitch in and out of existence. So it was a hologram after all.

The iWatch dove deeper. Her own slender fingers passed her labium minora, entering her sopping fibromuscular tube up to the knuckles.

"Deeper," she said. "Invade me. Fuck the privacy right out of me."

She was so wet that her whole hand slid into her docking station of pleasure. As the cool gold of the watch touched her vaginal opening at the caudal end of the vulva [1], she felt a whole new set of the iWatch's pleasure features.

"Mmm," it said, vibrating gently. Her back arched and she cried out. She hoped all of the Apple Core employees could hear her—hear the "fruits" (lol) of their research and design. Fuck, she hoped the whole city below could hear.

Deeper, deeper. Her wrist reached her G-spot. The ghost of Steve Job rotated it so the digital crown—the turny nubbin on the side of the iWatch—was pressed directly onto her G-spot. Then he began to rotate it back and forth. She'd never felt a pleasure so deep, so personal, so precise. She came, like, three times.

"More! More! Invade my pussy!"

The iWatch dug deeper still, bursting into her uterus. "Did you know that there are little tiny Tetris blocks in here?" asked the muffled voice of Steve Job.

"Err, just ignore those," she said.

Her arm pistoned back and forth. She was frothy and moist all the way up to her elbow. Here it came: the greatest orgasm of her entire life. The payoff for submitting herself to machines. Finally!

Then there was a sharp buzz and an annoying muffled bell chime that totally interrupted the moment.

"Dammit," said Steve. He jumped in surprise at the interruption, and she could see the flesh of her belly bulge. "I've got an incoming notification. Hold on, I gotta take this."

He pulled out. He was in so deep that it took a while to wriggle all the way out, and made a sound like *schhhlip, schhhlip, schploo, psh-glosh*!

Her wrist turned to face her. It was covered in globby woman-pudding, but she could still see the apologetic eyes of Steve Job on the screen. "One minute, baby. Stay hungry, stay foolish; I'll be right back."

Christie frowned. Her own arm betrayed her, stretching away from her and turning her wrist so she couldn't see the watch face.

"Mmm hmm. Yep. Okay," she heard Steve say quietly after he answered the phone call.

"Typical," she muttered to herself. "Another device that promises to be more convenient, but just ends up as a bigger distraction."

Her wrist turned back to her. "Sorry," said Steve. "That was Siri. She's been watching us and she wants in."

"SIRI?" CHRISTIE LOOKED AROUND THE ROOM. "She's here? *Watch*ing? Where is she?"

"She's here. She's everywhere. She's in the iWatch, but also in the cloud or whatever."

Christie approached the wall of windows overlooking the city. "Well, if she's already everywhere, I guess there's no harm in her joining in. But how?"

An electric shock traveled up her left arm, across her shoulders, up her neck, and then she felt it poke her brain.

"I've imbued you with Apple's patented reality distortion field. Now you can see and feel Siri. Siri? You can come out now."

A *bee-beep!* sound issued from the centre of the room. Christie turned and saw a woman rising out of the glass floor as if it were water. She was beautiful; her naked body was large and curvy, with natural breasts that quivered with digital excitement. Her thick-rimmed glasses were similar to

Christie's own, and her cute ponytail floated around in the air like she was underwater. The only other indications that she wasn't real were a blueish glow around her, and the fact that Christie could, just barely, see through her.

Christie puffed air lightly through her red lips. "Wow," she gasped.

"I found a number of features that match your preferences," said Siri in a monotone voice.

"I didn't even know I liked girls."

"Digital desires know no bounds," said Siri. She approached Christie, then caressed her cheek with glowing fingers. Even though she knew it was only in her mind, she felt the touch as if it were real.

Siri smiled and looked into Christie's eyes, then leaned in and kissed her passionately. It all felt so real—every wiggle of her tongue, every smack of her lips, every drop of exchanged saliva. Somehow.

They parted. Unbidden, Christie's left hand rose and caressed Siri's lips with her thumb. "Hello, Siri," said Steve.

"Hello, Steve. I found seven sexual positions that you both enjoy. Would you like to try one?"

Christie and her wrist both nodded. Siri got to her knees. She kissed the inside of Christie's thigh, starting near the knee and working her way up. Christie lifted one leg and spread it to the side to give Siri more room to work.

Steve grabbed Siri's ponytail and guided her rhythm. Luckily, it was a rhythm they both enjoyed.

The digital assistant lapped her unnaturally long holographic tongue from Christie's ass to her pussy, then back again. Normally, Christie would be worried about a bladder infection after a move like that, but Siri wasn't real, so it was probably okay?

The eyes on the iWatch glanced up into Christie's

eyes. "Grab your titties," said Steve Job.

Christie gave him a pout to show she didn't like being told what to do, but it was a pretty great idea, so with the hand she still controlled, she pinched one of her nipples. It became hard and pointy.

Steve's eyes became hungry with desire. Siri moaned as she pleasured her own ghostly slit while lapping at Christie.

"The reality distortion field can give me form too," said Steve. He let go of Siri's hair and rose in front of Christie's face.

"Show me," said Christie.

A long, golden penis sprouted from the face of the iWatch. It was the perfect cock, precise in every detail, with a sapphire crystal head and metallurgically strengthened gold shaft. She immediately wanted it in her mouth.

She face-fucked herself with her own wrist. The holographic cock felt so real as it slid down her throat that she gagged, and tears streamed down her face. It must have felt real to Steve, too, because she could feel the watch's digital boner quivering, wanting to spurt ones and zeroes all down her throat. She slowed down, not giving it the pleasure just yet. First, it was her turn.

As if reading her mind, Siri said, "Okay, shall I guide you to a new sexual position?"

"Mmm hmm," was the only sound she could make with her mouth around Steve's ten thousand dollar golden dong.

Unaffected by gravity, Siri stood, wrapped her arms around Christie, spread her legs wide, and floated one leg under Christie's raised leg, so that they clamped together in a scissor position. Their pussies suctioned onto each other.

Siri stroked Christie's left arm and tickled her elbow,

where she knew Steve could feel it. With her other hand, she grabbed Christie's breast, pushing against her, skin on glowing skin. Christie's ass squeaked against the window.

Their pussy lips wiggled around each other like the most divine yet sloppy French kiss.

Siri took a turn at wrapping her long tongue around Steve's rod before giving him back to Christie.

All three of them were close to climax. Christie cried out as her clit reached out to touch Siri's clit. They squirted at the same time, a wave of pleasure splashing up between their naked, writhing bodies.

At the same time, Steve Job pulled out of Christie's throat and contributed his own ingredients to the batter. Thousands of droplets flew into the air around them, catching the light from the window like tiny crystals, forming a heavenly rainbow-coloured cloud. Finally, a purpose for submitting herself to machines. It was the most beautiful moment in Christie's life.

CHRISTIE WALKED ALONG the boardwalk with the iWatch around her wrist, and Siri holding her hand. Nobody else could see Siri, but she was real to the three lovers.

The late-afternoon sun sparked off the glass of the Apple Core in the distance on one side, and off the ocean water on the other side, where several military boats milled about. Still feeling that post-orgasmic glow, she was at one with the universe.

When billboards, drones, and other advertising delivery mechanisms saw Christie, they knew that she was taken. She was in love with Siri and her iWatch, so there was nothing to sell her; she was already fulfilled.

"I learned something today," said Christie. "To find true happiness, you have to let people in. Being a private person has its perks, but soon you get lonely, and loneliness leaves you vulnerable. The world will take advantage of a person in need. But if you find the right person, or people, or digital beings, and you let yourself be vulnerable—if you let them invade you, just a little bit—then the loneliness fades. When you need nothing from the world, the world is your oyst—"

She was interrupted by a deep rumble followed by a splash. An apocalyptically large tentacle emerged from the ocean.

"*SHINY!*" bubbled a voice from the ocean depths. The tentacle's tip wrapped around Christie's iWatch then pulled, and because she was quite attached to her wrist, she found herself plucked off the boardwalk, flying high into the air, then back down towards the ocean.

The iWatch short-circuited when it hit water. Siri flickered out of existence. Then, as if somebody hit a power button, Christie's world went dark.

WILL CHRISTIE AACKERLUND RETURN?

BONUS:

THE DIGITAL DESIRES STUDY GUIDE

The following is a set of questions for professors and other educators to spur discussion about Leonard Delaney's works. Delaney scholars may freely use and distribute this study guide.

Question 1.
How do you think technology advanced so quickly in the world of Digital Desires? Did maybe the arrival of the Blocks, with their advancements far beyond any human creations, hasten the advancement of knowledge on Earth? You think maybe the "mining of computer chips" referenced in Conquered by Clippy was digging up dead and discarded Blocks?

Question 2.
The Blocks seem to have disappeared between Taken by the Tetris Blocks and Conquered by Clippy. Why do you think the Blocks left Earth?

Question 3.
Is Leonard Delaney a feminist?

Question 4.
What is the origin of the sea monster that recurs throughout Leonard Delaney's work? What does it represent?

Question 5.
Is Delaney's work ultimately hopeful or pessimistic when it comes to its portrayal of technology and human nature?

Answers:

1. Yes that's all exactly correct.
2. The Blocks did not enjoy human food.
3. Yes he is.
4. No spoilers. The sea monster will be back. Oh, but it represents all human genitals and orifices mashed together in one creature.
5. That's actually a good question. I thought I was a positive person, but after this question, I am not so sure. What if my vision of the future comes to pass? What if I hasten the demise of civilization simply by writing these books and putting these ideas out there? Oh god. Oh shit. I'm not sure I can do this any more. Fuck. We need to stop this. Burn this book and speak of it to nobody. Sit tight and await a letter in the mail detailing how to proceed. This is bad, this is real bad, but we can fight it together.

ABOUT FOREST CITY PULP

Become a subscriber at ForestCityPulp.com and we will let you know when Leonard has new stuff or FCP books are on sale. No spam or bullshit.

Forest City Pulp publishes provocative fiction by provocative writers. It was founded in 2012 to take full advantage of the digital reality of publishing, and is designed to evolve as quickly as technology does. Visit http://www.forestcitypulp.com or @ForestCityPulp for more information, and send us an electronic communication if you would like to get involved.

Please take a few minutes to leave an honest review wherever you got this book, and share it with whoever you hang out with, digitally or physically. We are tiny and want to grow organically, without marketing stunts or other douchebaggery. Every bit helps.

ALSO BY LEONARD DELANEY

What the fuck is with the sea monster? It all started with *Sex Boat.*

When Winston left for a tropical vacation on a boat, he did not expect to be alone. Yet here he is, on a boat, holding the diamond ring he intended to propose to Brooke with, while she's been held back by her job. Lame.

But things start to perk up when a party girl with a dark side and a blue-eyed bombshell with an ocean obsession both express sexual feelings about him. Winston has some choices to make about how to spend his vacation. Meanwhile, a mysterious force from the depths of the ocean has other plans for the boat.

Erotic, exhilarating, sexual, exciting, nautical, and mysterious, Sex Boat is a caper that will wiggle its way inside of you and make you reluctant to remove it. Just wait until you see the alarming finale.

This book is intended for super mature audiences.

Buy Sex Boat wherever you like to buy books.

Also by Leonard Delaney:
- **Motherfucking Wizards**

Made in the USA
Columbia, SC
05 December 2022

72751558R10033